ENCHANTING EVER AFTER

ENCHANTING EVER AFTER

AN ENDURING LEGACY NOVELLA

DAWN BROWER

AMANDA MARIEL

*For everyone still waiting for their happily-ever-after.
Don't lose hope, it might yet arrive.*

"It isn't what we say or think that defines us,
but what we do."

— JANE AUSTEN, SENSE AND
SENSIBILITY

CONTENTS

ONE ENCHANTING KISS
Amanda Mariel

CHARMING HER ROGUE
ENDURING LEGACY 10

CHAPTER 1

April 1629

Samuel Noble didn't trust many people, and most of the ones he did were his family. His entire life had been one lie after the next. No one, save his family, actually knew his real identity. They kept that secret out of necessity. To admit to anyone, his true name might mean his death.

His father, along with his two aunts, had been executed as witches. In a time when every slight could end in a witch trial, they had lost. His mother, Ailis, had been pregnant with him when they had murdered his father. If his Uncle Daniel and his mother hadn't taken the children away from New Berwick, Scotland, thirty-seven years earlier, they would have all perished. He had no doubt the rest of his family would have died in the same way his father, Baron Niall Dalais, had—burned at the stake.

Anger surged through him at the thought of the fate he'd escaped—at the danger that constantly followed his family, and all they'd suffered.

They'd hidden in France for years, before fleeing to London. Samuel had worked hard to make his fortune as a common man. Claiming he was of noble birth would not have helped him, and with James the VI still on the throne, it could have lead to an execution of his entire family. That was not a risk he'd been willing to take. Samuel had to protect what was left of his family.

His circumstances might change though...

"What are ye going tae do?" Daniel asked His Scottish accent was thick as he spoke. Samuel had never lived in Scotland and had easily slipped into English society, and the accent that came with it. He'd been determined to never stand out or catch anyone's unwanted attention. His Uncle Daniel had married Samuel's mother years ago. Another necessary decision he'd made, along with Samuel's mother to protect the family. They created a family for Samuel and his cousins, Lachlan, Moire, and Lili. Daniel was the only father that Samuel had known, but he knew who had sired him, and he knew his birth right.

"I'm not sure it is wise to come forward now." Samuel tapped his finger restlessly on the wooden table in his office. He owned a shipping company that often traveled to Bombay and Calcutta. Trading in those areas could be exceedingly perilous; as well as, have equally high profit margins.

He might be considered common now, but his wealth attracted women of the higher class. Though he doubted any of those high-born ladies would deign to marry him, they did welcome him into their bed and gladly took the trinkets he purchased for them. "We're happy. Why should I try to regain my father's titles and lands now?"

"Because it is yer birthright," Daniel explained. "And the climate of the country is no the same as it was under James' rule. His son is no as inclined tae hunt down witches and execute them. He's more interested in money, and his arguments with parliament led to him dissolving it. He'll need funds to find money through nonparliamentary means. This is the best opportunity you have. Wave yer wealth at him and he'll gladly hand ye what rightfully belongs tae ye."

He hated what the deceased king had done to his father. His family's gifts did not mean they were witches or worshiped evil. Sometimes Samuel was embarrassed by the gifts passed down in his blood. He didn't want anyone to know that he had the same ability as his father. Being able to see colors around a person and know when they lied, were happy, or in love...it was his curse.

He used it mercilessly, though, and that gift had helped him thrive as a shipping magnate. Conflicted, he reached up to massage his temples.

Admitting that aloud would be his undoing, and he did not have any wish to die. "The current king might not be concerned with witchcraft but I have little doubt he'd happily hang me and steal from my coffers to fund his endeavors if he knew the truth about my family."

"I said tae request yer land and title back," Daniel began. "No tae confess all the family secrets. I'm no a bloody fool, and I dinna expect ye to be either."

Samuel scrubbed his hands over his face and blew out a fortifying breath. Perhaps Daniel had the right of it. The Dalais lands belonged to him and he should try to retrieve them from the crown.

He would have to be wise about it, though. He couldn't waltz into the throne room and wave a gold-filled sack as a white flag of surrender, then expect King Charles to give into his demands. This would have to be handled with finesse. He would need an emissary. "Who do we trust to go to the king on my behalf?" he asked.

"Moire's husband might negotiate on yer behalf," Daniel offered. Thomas Astley had married Moire almost two decades ago. All their children were nearly grown now. Still, he couldn't risk their safety. Samuel had never married. He hadn't wanted to risk a woman's life by tying his life to hers, and he didn't even want to think of children. Instead he adored all the children his cousins brought into the world.

"That's putting the family in harm's way. We need someone that can deliver a message from me, without giving the king my identity as Samuel Noble on the chance he wishes to execute us." He ran his hand through his golden blond hair in frustration. "We're going to have to use a paid messenger, and have someone that is not connected to me directly give the missive to the messenger to deliver. It would be better if it appeared it came from France instead of England too. Let the king believe we never returned and have lived in France this entire time."

"Staying alive has always been a priority," Daniel agreed. "I have a suggestion if yer willing tae listen."

Listening rarely posed a risk. "Tell me."

"I'll sail with one of yer vessels on its next voyage. Have it make a stop in France on its return voyage and sell some of its cargo there. The letter can be given to the captain from a messenger in France tae be delivered tae the King, from one of our friends there."

"You've already considered this, haven't you?" Samuel should have realized his uncle would have thought of everything. Not once in all of his thirty-seven years had Daniel ever failed him. "The answer can be sent to them, then they can forward it to us."

"I'll stay behind," Daniel said. "Let the ship return

without me tae England, then when the King responds I can deliver it tae ye myself."

He hated that Daniel would have to remain in France. There was no other way to guarantee this didn't touch his family, though. "All right. We'll try to get the Dalais Barony and name restored."

"Glad ye are willing tae try," Daniel replied. "I'll start preparations. Inform me when yer ship will sail, and I'll complete my part."

"I trust you will," Samuel said. "But above all, please take care. I don't wish to lose you if this turns sour."

"I'll return. Ye may count on that." Daniel nodded and then turned to leave Samuel alone in his office.

Samuel hoped he didn't come to regret this decision. He would love to restore his father's good name, but his remaining family's lives were not worth losing to ensure that outcome. He had to have faith in Daniel, and that it would all go as they had planned. Samuel couldn't accept anything else.

TEMPERANCE WARREN LOUNGED IN THE PARLOR HER mind wandering as she stared out the window and waited for her father to speak. She didn't belong at court and she didn't belong amongst the common people. She did not truly belong anywhere, and the knowledge stung.

Her father was the Earl of Lennox. She was his bastard daughter. He had claimed her as his ward, but everyone knew the truth. They said nothing in her presence. No, they would never do that. It would upset the earl, and result in losing the earl's favor, also in most instances, the favor of the king.

Her father was one of the king's favorites, and as long as that remained true, the courtiers accepted her. Most of the time... Temperance had no friends or confidants. She couldn't trust anyone, not even her father. She always had to be on guard because one misstep, and she'd be no better than a pauper. Her father expected her to remain pure and not embarrass him. Temperance would not disappoint him. Not because she loved the earl, but because she feared him.

"Temperance," her father said. "Are you listening to me?"

"Yes," she replied in a calm, even tone. It did not do well to show any sort of emotion with him. He hated what he called histrionics. "You wished to speak to me about my future."

He lifted his lips into a smile. "Yes, we need to secure you a match. It is pastime you married."

Temperance swallowed hard. She had turned twenty a fortnight ago. This conversation didn't surprise her. The fact her father hadn't already betrothed her to a man did. "Of course," she replied demurely. She hated that she had to act obedient. It hurt her deep down to hide her emotions, but the pain would be far worse if her father beat her. It had taken once for that to happen and she had learned to pretend to be the obedient daughter. It helped that in most instances it was true, and she didn't dare defy him. "Have you found someone to marry?"

"I am to speak to the king about it." He leaned back against his chair and steepled his fingers together. "He'll find you a proper match. One that benefits the crown, and the earldom."

But not one that she might find favorable... Temperance's fate was not to be one she would choose. She had never been given any choices. Why should that change when it came time to find a husband? "I trust the king's judgement."

King Charles would do whatever he thought best for him. He wouldn't care one bit what Temperance might want, or what the man he forced to marry her hoped for. It would not be a good marriage. Her chest squeezed at the knowledge. She didn't trust any man with her fortunes. Sometimes she wished she'd never been born. This was no life for a woman. How could a man accept her, being illegitimate, and not be at least tempted to treat her terribly?

"It is wise of you to leave these decisions to the men in your life. I'm glad you are not going to be difficult." He tapped his foot against the floor. "After the king chooses your husband, we'll make wedding arrangements. Your betrothal is one of my highest priorities. It might take a while for the king to find the right gentleman, but I have faith he will."

Temperance would not roll her eyes. She wouldn't. That would only ensure that her father smacked her, or worse. She forced a smile onto her face. There was nothing else she could do. Except run, but to what end? Where would she go, and how would she provide for herself? Women had few choices, and the ones they did have were terrible. "I'll pray tonight for the king. He has many decisions, and it cannot be easy for him to make the right ones." She'd pray he took many, many months to secure a betrothal for her. The current king was the type to sell her to the highest bidder. Money meant more to King Charles than the subjects he ruled. What sort of man would claim a bastard as a bride?

"I'm glad I was blessed with such a thoughtful, obedient daughter." Her father nearly beamed in pleasure. His dark hair had gone to gray at the sides. She'd never known her mother, but she'd been told that she had fair skin and pale blonde hair. Temperance had her father's coloring. There was no denying his blood ran through her veins. Even if it sickened her a little to admit it. "I'll leave you to your meditations. I'll return once I have more to share." Her mother's death left a hole in her life that could never be filled. She mourned that loss every day.

"I'll patiently await your return." Temperance

bowed her head. "Safe travels, my lord." She could never refer to him as father. He expected formality and discretion. It suited her, for Temperance hated him too much to call him by the honorific. Still, she pretended to honor him in order to safeguard herself. She might have wished never to have been born, but she still did what was necessary to survive. She glanced upward as he stood.

"Farewell, Temperance." Her father nodded at her. "Prepare yourself for marriage. When I return, it will be time to say your vows."

She prayed the man the king chose was amiable and didn't believe in beating his wife. None the less, her expectations were low. It would be wonderful if she could come to love her husband, but fate hadn't been kind to her so far. It was bound to disappoint her in this as well...

CHAPTER 2

July 1629

The Palace of Whitehall had more than fifteen hundred rooms, and Temperance found it easy to become lost navigating all the corridors. She did not want to be at the palace, and she definitely had no desire to meet with King Charles.

Life at court could be treacherous, and avoiding being caught in the web of deceit often proved difficult. Her father slid into court life with an ease only a snake could achieve. He thrived on subterfuge and schemes. Such was not a skill Temperance wished to emulate.

The earl's friendship with King Charles was one that he'd cultivated and utilized at every opportunity.

But the King had proved difficult with the earl's latest desires.

He'd been trying to convince the king to secure a match for Temperance, but the king continued to delay doing so. Temperance enjoyed the freedom that provided her. As long as she was not betrothed, she could breathe a little easier and stay in comfort at her father's home. That freedom ended when she'd been summoned to Whitehall.

She had arrived at the palace a sennight ago and had not yet been in the King's presence. Of course that could not last. The king wanted her in the throne room so he could have a look at her. She was not to speak unless the king asked her a direct question. Her father had explained that her opinion did not matter, and that she was to remain demure and agreeable. She was not to insult the king, and if she did, she would be punished.

"Pardon me," she asked a woman she encountered in the corridor. "Could you please help me?"

"What is it you need, girl?" Her hair was covered entirely and wrinkles had formed at the corner of her mouth and eyes. She wore all black and had a stern expression on her face. "Speak. I cannot wait on you all day."

"My apologies..." She cleared her throat. "I'm lost. Could you direct me to the throne room?" Her hand shook a little, so she brought both her hands together in front of her. Temperance didn't want the woman to realize how frightened she made her feel. Why did she have to be at the palace? She prayed her father would send her home soon.

"You're not as lost as you believe." She pointed to a corridor behind her. "Go left there, then straight down until you reach a set of double doors. There are guards outside that will admit you when the king is ready for you."

"Thank you," she said in as humble a tone as she could manage, then curtsied. She moved past the older woman and followed her directions to the throne room. There were guards there, as the woman had mentioned. "The king has sent for me."

"Your name?" one of them asked.

"Temperance Warren," she said. Her voice wobbled a little as she spoke her name.

"Wait here," he told her and then went inside. He came back a few moments later, but it had seemed like forever. "You may go inside."

There were several men inside the throne room, but no other ladies. That wasn't always how things were, from what Temperance understood. Women were welcome in the throne room, but usually when the queen was also present. Today it seemed as if the queen didn't want to take part in this council or hadn't been invited. All the men had grave expressions on their faces. A shiver of trepidation made the hairs at her nape stand on end. Temperance did not want any part of whatever made them appear so somber. And yet, she had no choice.

She curtsied. "Your Grace."

"Come forward so I can see you." He waved at her. She was nothing more than chattel to be sold off in service of her father and her king. Temperance understood her place in the world. That didn't mean she had to like it.

Hiding her distaste, she did as the king instructed. He stared at her for several uncomfortable moments. Her father stood off to the side in silence. He had glared at her when she'd dared to address the king. She realized her mistake immediately, but could not take the words back.

Her cheeks warmed. She'd be slapped for her impertinence later.

"Her visage is passable," the king said. "I am certain I can find a man willing to take her on. I cannot make any promises." He rubbed his chin thoughtfully, then picked up a missive from a nearby table. "Though there might be someone who isn't in a position to say no."

"Your Grace..." Her father began to speak. "Surely, you are not considering that man."

"You wish your daughter to marry gentry, do you not?" The king raised an eyebrow. "This man is that and he will not be so choosy as some. He'll accept your bastard if he hopes to regain his title and lands."

Her father clenched his hands into fists. "He's not good enough for Temperance."

"Temperance isn't good enough for anyone else," the king retorted. "It's this man or none."

Temperance wished she had the choice of adding her opinion to the discussion. Who was this man, and why did her father object to him so forcefully? Was he a horrid man, or did her father dislike him because his rank wasn't high enough? She had many questions, but uncovering the answers might prove difficult.

The earl took several deep breaths. He was attempting to control his temper. Yelling at the king would not endear the sovereign to his plight. Neither would the king change his mind. "All right. I accept your decision. Temperance will marry Baron Dalais."

Her father had a pained expression on his face. He clearly did not like conceding to the king's decision.

"Have faith, Lennox. Dalais will be good for your daughter, and if he remains loyal, perhaps I'll gift him with a more prestigious title. That should make you happy." The king chuckled lightly. "It will make me exceedingly delighted to inform the baron he may have his lands and title back for a price. A marriage, and fine. A hefty one. My coffers need funds."

Temperance didn't care one whit if her father

was happy. She had to discern why he had been so adamantly against this baron. What made him so unfavorable?

"You may go, Temperance." Her father waved her off. "You're not needed for the rest of this discussion. Stay in your chambers for now."

She turned away from them and left the room. There was much to think about and to prepare for. If she was to marry, she had to find a way to accept it. She'd go from one man's power and into another's, and she didn't know how she felt about it. No, that wasn't true. She did know, and she hated it. That didn't change her fate.

THREE WEEKS LATER...

The bloody bastard had conditions. Of course, he did. Samuel should have expected nothing less from an English king. They were selfish but claimed to have the people's best interests at heart. He wasn't sure the price the king asked was worth it. Not the money... Samuel didn't care about the money. He had expected the king to ask for a tidy sum. It was the other part he had an issue with. He had decided to never marry and now the king was demanding it of him. And to a girl several years younger than him. It didn't seem right.

"What is bothering ye?" Daniel asked.

Samuel tossed the missive across the table in his office. He'd spent many hours there instead of at his modest home. There was always something that needed his attention, and it helped to be close to the shipping yard. He had been all right with staying in his office. Until the missive had arrived and destroyed his ability to see reason. "Read that."

Daniel picked up the missive and scanned it. "This is good news." He waved it at Samuel. "The king has agreed tae yer request. Ye can get yer land and title back."

"He expects me to marry this Temperance Warren chit," Samuel said in a scathing tone. "You know how I feel about marriage."

"Come now lad, ye didn't think that ye could get yer land and title back and remain unmarried?" Daniel shook his head. "The barony needs an heir. Otherwise what is the point of gaining the land back only tae have it fall empty again?"

"I have heirs," Samuel told him. "My cousins..."

"Are no a direct line tae the title. They're through yer aunts. The crown will no accept them as ye well know."

Samuel scowled. He didn't want to admit that his uncle was right. The king wouldn't accept them. He was barely accepting Samuel now, and if he wanted his lands back, he would have to give in to what the king demanded of him.

He would have to marry the girl; however, he

didn't have to like it. Perhaps he wouldn't consummate the marriage. Even if he needed heirs as Daniel reminded him... Did he really want to have children and put them at risk? What if the climate in England changed again, and they were persecuted? It all seemed too dangerous.

He sighed.

"Do you really believe this is a wise decision? We're happy all being together in England. No one knows who we are. What if they discover that we all survived?" He hated this, and yes, he was frightened. Samuel didn't want to bring any calamity on his family's heads.

Still, something deep inside demanded he reclaim all that his father had lost. He blew out a deep breath before continuing, "If you are all right with this, and what it might potentially bring upon us all, I'll write the king and accept his concessions."

"I dinna wish fer ye tae do anything ye are no comfortable with," Daniel began. "But aye, I do believe this is the best thing ye can do, fer yerself, and the family. So much was taken from ye all. It might help them, and it is your birthright. That land should have always been yers."

Samuel nodded. "You are right, of course you are." He blew out a breath. "The lands should never have been stripped from my family, and my father and aunts should not have been burned on a pyre." He closed his eyes and fought his emotions.

It still choked him up to think about what had happened to them. The pain and agony they must have suffered. Not only on that pyre as they burned alive, but the weeks of torture as they were on trial. "I cannot change the fate they were dealt, but I can regain what belongs to my family. I will have to keep our secret. This woman the king demands I marry..." He opened his eyes and met Daniel's gaze. "She must never know that our gifts, our curse, still resides within us. It's the only way I can protect my cousins, and their children."

"Shouldn't she know?" Daniel raised an eyebrow. "If ye have children..."

Samuel shook his head. "If the day arrives that I have a child, and he or she shows they have one of the three gifts I'll reconsider." He tapped his foot impatiently. "But until then, for our continued survival, no one must speak of it in her presence."

Daniel rubbed his face with his hands. "I understand yer reluctance, and I must agree with it. We dinna know if she will be trustworthy. I'll inform everyone so they know not to mention their gifts."

"I'll write to the king immediately." Samuel sat back at his desk and slid parchment in front of him. He slipped his quill into the inkpot and began writing. "When it is completed, will you see it delivered?"

"Aye," Daniel responded. "Do ye wish to use the same subterfuge?"

"No," Samuel said. "We can pretend I've returned

to England, and have a messenger here deliver it; however, ensure it is one located near the docks. That will make it appear as if I sent it as I arrived."

"I'll handle it myself," Daniel replied.

Samuel finished writing the missive. He accepted the king's terms and said he would present himself to court in a sennight to prepare for his wedding. It didn't sit well in his gut, but he sealed his fate when he signed the missive and handed it to Daniel. Soon he'd be a married man, and he would have one more person to protect.

God help him.

CHAPTER 3

One month later...

It was her wedding day. Temperance had not met her intended. She was to go to the altar without even being introduced to him. She didn't know if he was old, fat, or if his overall demeanor was revolting. It would be too much to ask for a handsome and kind man. Her luck did not sway in that direction. Everything went wrong in her life. Of course this would as well.

It did not bode well for her marriage that they had not been allowed to meet before they said reciting their vows. The contracts had been drawn and signed, and her dowry had been given to the king, along with whatever fine the king demanded of her betrothed for the return of his land and title.

Temperance didn't have friends or allies. She had

no one to ask about her future husband. There had been many whispers when people noticed her. They were talking about her and her betrothed. When she neared, they would all become silent, but as soon as she passed them, the whispers began again. She learned to hide from their view so she might eavesdrop on the rumors they shared.

She hadn't been able to learn everything about her husband-to-be; however, she had discovered the reason her father hadn't been keen on her marriage to Baron Dalais. His father had been executed as a witch. It was scandalous, and the reason for all the whispering. She would marry into a family that had tainted blood. Were the rumors of their abilities true? Had his father actually worshiped evil? She always had questions and no answers for them.

"Pardon me," a lady said as she entered the room. "My name is Mary and I've been tasked with helping you prepare for your wedding."

Temperance sighed. It was time to embrace her fate. Perhaps once she was alone with her intended, he'd explain to her about his family. "Very well," she told Mary. "Please come forward so we may begin."

She bathed in water scented with rose petals. Her hair was washed, then plaited into an intricate chignon at the nape of her neck. Tiny seed pearls were affixed into her hair, and a diadem placed on top of her head. Her gown had been designed in a simple style with billowing sleeves. The color was a rich blue, and the material silk and velvet. It was the prettiest gown she'd ever owned. Her father had taken her in, but he hadn't given her every luxury.

She held no illusions. This gown had been created for appearances. The earl had wanted to give the impression of his enormous generosity to his bastard daughter.

"You're ready," the lady declared. "And may I say how lovely you look. That gown is perfect for you."

Temperance stood still in the middle of her assigned chamber. She didn't know how to converse with anyone. Her father had strict rules for her and she feared if she said something incorrect, her father would learn of it and punish her. Soon she would be married, and she didn't know what that might bring her. Her husband could be of a similar ilk as her father. It scarcely signified because until she said her vows, her father could still discipline her. "Thank you," she replied in a reserved tone.

"Do you know what is expected of you?" Mary asked.

She always knew what was expected of her. The earl had ensured she would always do what he wanted. Her father had arranged this marriage, and he would be disappointed if somehow it did not happen. Temperance would ensure it did, for that reason alone. She did not want to incur the earl's wrath. Instead of telling the lady all of that, she asked, "What do you believe is expected of me?"

Mary stepped forward and placed her hand on Temperance's "Do you understand what I am asking you?"

Temperance had missed having her mother in her life every day, but no more than she did in this moment. She would have loved to have someone who truly cared for her with her as she prepared to say her vows. A mother that would hold her and tell her that she deserved happiness, and to tell her how marriage could be a good thing.

Sorrow swelled within Temperance. Her mother never had a chance to live. She'd died in childbirth before she had seen her twentieth year. Temperance had caused her mother's death. The earl did not have a care for her mother as he already had a wife and heir. Her mother had been a mere dalliance and soon forgotten as if she were nothing.

At least Temperance would have the sanctity of marriage if she were to die giving birth to her husband's child. "You are asking if I understand that I must obey my husband in all things."

"Yes," Mary replied. "And do you understand your duty to your husband?"

"I do," she said. "I must lie with him and bear him a child. He needs heirs." Temperance stated it as a fact, because it was, and there was no escaping it. She had no emotion in her voice. There was no room for feelings. It would not help her. The wedding would go as planned, and soon she would be free of her father. She hoped that in that freedom she would not find another prison.

"You do understand," Mary replied. She nodded her head. "Come. It's time to go."

They left the chamber and walked through the corridors until they reached the chapel located on the grounds of Whitehall. Her father waited for her at the entrance. "Are you prepared to do your duty?" he asked.

"I am," she said in a firm tone.

"Good." He left her and went inside the chapel. Mary walked with her inside and stood with her at the beginning of the aisle. She strolled down and took a seat in one of the pews, then Temperance followed. She stopped once she reached her intended.

Temperance turned to face him and had to withhold a gasp. He wasn't old or fat. This man was perfect, with golden hair and sapphire blue eyes. He was tall, lean, and the handsomest man she'd ever laid eyes upon. His visage was appealing; however, that did not mean his heart was kind. In time she'd learn that, but at least he wouldn't be difficult to gaze upon.

SAMUEL STARED DOWN AT HIS BRIDE AND HELD BACK A frown. She was young, but he'd known that. Her hair was dark and her eyes a silvery gray that shined with emotions. Her face lacked expression, but she couldn't hide her feelings from him. The poor lass was frightened. He didn't know if it was of him, her father, the king, or all three. She hadn't been given any more of a choice than he had.

He felt like a right arse...

They were in this situation together, and he would do his best to protect her. After this farce of a wedding was finished, they would leave and return to Scotland. Perhaps once they were married he could calm her fears.

He'd paid the king's tithe and once his vows were said, he'd have everything back. The sum the king had demanded hadn't been as much as Samuel had expected. It hadn't put a dent in his own coffers. He'd be able to restore the Dalais land to its former glory, and with luck, win his wife's loyalty and friendship—if not her heart.

He prayed he didn't regret this choice.

"Now that the bride is here, we may begin," the vicar declared.

Samuel said his vows, but he didn't really feel any of them. His bride did the same, but her voice shook as she spoke. What had this woman endured? She was a frightened little rabbit, and her aura was a mixture of colors. Most of them were not good—she was fairly brimming in sorrow and fear, but the whole of her couldn't be determined by those emotions alone.

He could never explain to her how he understood her emotions and fears. It would only serve to terrify her more. One thing shined brighter than her fears—her innocence mixed with her strength of will. She was lovely, too. He hoped they could find something to connect with or their marriage wouldn't have anything to sustain it.

"What God has joined together may no man put asunder," the vicar said. "I present to you the Baron and Baroness Dalais."

He was married. Samuel didn't feel tied to another person, but he supposed that was to be expected. This wasn't a marriage bound in love, but separate duties—he to his birthright and she to her father. They had nothing to truly bind them together. Perhaps, in time, they would.

"Lady Dalais," he said, and held his arm out to her.

She lifted her hand and placed it on his arm, and then they strolled down the aisle. There was to be a wedding breakfast. Samuel wished he could skip it and take his new bride to his London home. It was too soon to depart for Scotland. He made plans to leave in a few days, but for the moment, at least they would not have to remain at Whitehall under the king's thumb.

"My lord," she said in a quiet tone.

"You do not need to be so formal with me," he said in a calm tone. He didn't wish to frighten her further. "My name is Samuel. Please use my given name."

She licked her lips, and Samuel wished he didn't find it enticing. He desired her more than he expected he would. He might not be able to keep his distance from her. Still, he would not rut with her like a wild animal. They should become more acquainted before considering something as intimate as the marriage bed, and if he consummated his marriage, he'd have to be careful. He hadn't decided if he wanted to bring children into the world, and he didn't want any accidents because he could not control his needs.

"Samuel," she said in that same mumbled tone. "When we leave here..."

"We'll go to my home here in London." She wanted to know more about him and what their life would be like. "Then we'll go to Scotland."

She nodded. "I didn't realize you had a home in London. Was that part of the lands restored to you?"

His wife was inquisitive, but also seemed uncertain she should ask these questions. He was amused, but didn't wish to hurt her fragile feelings by laughing. She wouldn't know these things about him. The king sure as hell didn't, and he wanted to keep it that way. "Not exactly," he said. "My lands associated with the title are all in Scotland." Samuel Noble owned the house in London. Samuel Dalais owned the title and lands in Scotland. In time he'd tell her that, but not with the king's gossips surrounding them.

"I thought you were in France," she said, then shook her head. "Forgive me, my lord. I shouldn't pry."

Samuel frowned. "It's not prying, but let's discuss this later. We have plenty of time to learn about each other."

He glanced around the banquet hall. They had arrived for the wedding breakfast and the room was filling fast. There was a table set for the bride and groom to sit alone, near the king and queen's table. Samuel hoped this farce ended fast, but he feared they would be there for many hours to come.

He blew out a breath and wished he had allowed his mother and Daniel to attend. They had both wanted to, but he had nixed the idea immediately. Their safety could not be assured if they had attended the wedding. It was far better for them to keep their distance.

"Temperance," he said. Samuel did not ask her permission to use her given name. She was his wife now and he would not stand on ceremony. "Would you be upset if we slipped out of the banquet hall and didn't stay for the meal?"

She shook her head. "No. I'd rather leave."

"Good." He grinned. Samuel had expected that

answer. "Then we'll send our regrets to the king. I'm sure he'll make me pay another fine for the slight, but the price will be worth it. I hate crowds."

She smiled for the first time since he saw her walking down the aisle. Her entire face lit up and made her even more beautiful. "I'm not fond of them either."

Samuel didn't wait for her to change her mind. Her belongings had already been instructed to be loaded onto his carriage, and they had no reason to remain at the palace. As far as Samuel was concerned, he had done his duty.

He'd married her.

No one said he would be required to break bread with the king, and he sure as hell was not inclined to do so. They both had smiles on their face as the carriage took them away from Whitehall. At least they had found one thing they agreed on, and Samuel counted that as a good start.

One month later...

Traveling from London to New Berwick had been exhausting. The Dalais lands were located outside of the Scottish village, but Samuel would hold no memories of the manor. He hadn't even been born there. His mother had given birth to him in France, far away from the people who wanted to murder his entire family. The carriage wheels rattled against the street as they rolled through the town, heading toward Dalais Manor.

Samuel had sent workers ahead when the king had agreed to restore his land. He expected the estate to be in disarray. It had been empty for almost three decades. When his family had made their escape, the villagers had stormed the manor to carry his father off to be put on trial for witchcraft. His mother had hid with his cousins until Daniel helped them escape. It had been a near thing, and if they had been discovered, all of them would have perished.

Thoughts of that night haunted him. He couldn't imagine what they had endured, and he likely never would. That didn't mean he couldn't picture their terror in his mind. He glanced at his wife. She'd been a timid little mouse and barely spoken to him since they said their vows.

He allowed her to have her privacy, and didn't make any demands on her. Once they were settled in Dalais Manor, he'd speak to her about what he expected of her. Temperance needed something to cling to, and her uncertain future continued to put her on edge. The colors swirling around her screamed at him, and for his own sanity, he had to help her calm her inner storm.

The carriage came to a stop in front of a large manor house. The men he'd hired had already started on repairs. The door had been replaced, along with several windows. Some villagers had been hired to clean the entire manor, so he hoped it was livable. The rest could wait. Temperance could redecorate, however she liked. All Samuel wanted was a functional estate and a bed to sleep in.

"It doesn't look too terrible," he mumbled.

"No, it does not."

He turned to meet her gaze. She rarely spoke, so

when she did it always caught him off guard. He tilted his lips upward into a warm smile. "Do you think you can be comfortable here?"

"I do," she said in a modest tone. It pained his heart a little how broken she seemed to be. "Do you believe you can?"

He shook his head. "I don't know. I suppose I can." It was still difficult for him to see this manor as his home, and he couldn't help thinking he might never see it that way. He hadn't grown up here, and he certainly didn't feel anything endearing toward the town that had turned on his family.

Reclaiming his lands and title had nothing to do with sentiment and everything to do with taking back what belonged to him. The act was as much for his father as it had been for himself. He might never feel comfortable here, but he could pretend to, leastwise for now.

After the estate was repaired and he was satisfied that it had been restored to its former glory, he'd return to London. That was where his true home and family were. If Temperance wanted to come with him, she could. He would let her decide where she belonged.

Samuel stepped out of the carriage and then turned to assist Temperance out. They walked into the manor together. There were little furnishings remaining inside, but it had been cleaned. He should have considered there would not be much there for them; however, that was a problem he could easily solve. "We might not have a bed. There might not be much furniture in the manor."

She shrugged. "We can explore and see what we discover." Temperance moved past him and went to the large staircase near the entrance. She moved up the stairs without saying a word.

Samuel fell into step behind her. If she wanted to explore, then he'd let her. The manor was almost as much of a mystery to him as it was to her. His mother had told him a bit about the house, but nothing compared to first hand knowledge.

They made it to the second story and wandered down the corridor. They went into the first bedchamber. There was a four-poster bed with what appeared to be an intact mattress and fresh bedding. When the villagers had cleaned, they must have anticipated the new lord and lady of the manor would need a bed.

"Do you think all the rooms are like this or just this one?" she asked. Temperance nibbled on her bottom lip, and it didn't take a man who could read auras to understand her fear. They hadn't shared a bed since they said their vows, and she didn't wish to now. He didn't blame her. They were only starting to know each other.

"Why don't we inspect each one and find out."

They did, and all the rooms were pristine, but only two had new mattresses. The Lord and Lady's chambers, which were connected by a door. The baroness's chamber was more delicate with pastel coloring. The first chamber they had entered had bolder colors, in rich reds and golds.

Temperance became more tranquil once she walked into the lady's chamber. "I suppose this is meant to be my room."

"If that is what you wish," he replied nonchalantly. "But if you're more comfortable in another room, you may move to it."

"Once we have more beds," she replied in a light tone.

He shrugged. "Or we could have some of the workers move this one. It's your decision."

She glanced up at him with a serious expression on her face. "Why are you so nice to me?"

It pained him to hear that question from her lips. "Has everyone been unkind to you?" No one should live in fear, and it was clear Temperance had never known a moment of true peace.

"Yes," she admitted. "Any kindness came with expectations. What do you want with me?"

He shook his head. "I want you to be happy."

It was a simple answer, but Samuel meant it. He didn't want Temperance to feel as if she owed him anything. She should do something for herself, something she had been denied, and in doing so perhaps she could finally relax. He hoped he could give that to her.

"No one has ever offered me that," she said in a quiet tone. "I am not sure what happiness is."

Samuel blew out a breath. "Then it's time you learned." He smiled. "Do whatever pleases you. I'm going to walk into town and see how the villagers react to me. I shouldn't be long." He turned on his heels and left her alone.

If he stayed a moment longer, he might do something foolish like kiss her. She wasn't ready for his advances.

TEMPERANCE STROLLED BESIDE SAMUEL THROUGH THE winding garden paths. She sneaked a glance at her husband, her heart fluttering. She had never been so confused in her entire life. Her husband had been good to her since the very beginning. He never raised his voice or chastised her. His home in London had been simple and elegant. She had her own bedchamber there, and not once had he visited her.

They had not consummated their marriage, and she couldn't help wondering why he hadn't wanted her in that way. Did he not find her desirable? The idea stung, but she also took comfort in the fact that he did not push her.

Of course, she was a contradiction. She both feared and desired for the night he joined her and made her his true wife. Some nights she wished he would join her for the sole purpose of finally having the deed completed. Other nights she was grateful for her solace.

She should ask him to join her, but she was afraid he might accept her invitation. What was wrong with her?

Temperance and Samuel had been at Dalais Manor for a month. The villagers were wary of them, but they hadn't outright snubbed them. The men and women who had been willing to persecute Samuel's family were either dead or too old to do anything of significance.

Not many of them fared well during the witch trials. Neighbor turned on neighbor and bred seeds of mistrust that lasted through the years. New Berwick was not a welcoming sort of village. Temperance didn't even try to make friends. It was a marvel Samuel had found staff for the manor.

She strolled through the garden relishing the feel of sun on her face. Samuel had hired a gardener to prune and plant where needed. Most of the stuff that was planted wouldn't grow until spring, but what was left in the garden had been tamed. It was Temperance's favorite area of the entire estate.

Samuel stared at a fountain that had been repaired. He had a frown on his face. Temperance had discovered she disliked seeing him unhappy. His kindness endeared him to her. "What is bothering you?"

He turned toward her and smiled. "Nothing." Samuel shook his head. "My mother loves this fountain. She told me how my father had it built for her."

Temperance frowned. "I didn't realize your mother was still alive." Samuel didn't talk about his family much. She wondered about them, of course, but didn't want him to feel obligated to share anything with her.

He sighed. "I don't like to talk about my family. But if you have questions, I will do my best to answer them."

"I shouldn't like to pry. However, I am curious how we came to be here…together."

"My uncle thought I should reclaim my title and lands." Samuel shrugged. "It's how we both ended up here. I listened to his advice."

"Do you regret that decision?" Temperance hadn't wanted to marry him, but now that she had she was glad for their union. He had wanted her to be happy, and slowly she had allowed herself to be. Samuel gave her the space to find her own way and let her enjoy life. Now she wanted happiness for him as well.

"I do not," he said. "I just miss my family. It's lonely here."

"Loneliness is all I've ever known," she said in a quiet tone. "It's safer that way."

Samuel frowned. "That is no way to live." He tilted his head to the side. "Your father was not good to you, was he?"

"No, he was not." It was her turn to frown. "He's not a good man. Unfortunately for me his status with the king has always been far more important than my welfare. I believe he saw to my needs as a way to further his own ambitions."

Samuel met her gaze. "He hoped for a better match for you than me. I'd wager he didn't expect the king to offer your hand in marriage to a man tainted by witchcraft."

"You would win that bet," she said, then smiled. "The king wasn't keen on making a match for me at all. From the whispers at court my father was lucky you decided to petition the king for your lands." She glanced away from him. "I'm fortunate as well. My life has been better with you." She did not add the qualifier that her father had been cruel. That part was understood.

"I think we will be fine together." He picked her hand up in his, then lifted it to his lips. Samuel kissed her palm. "We're friends are we not?"

That kiss sent tiny shivers down her spine. Desire pooled at her core, and she wanted him to press his lips to hers. She had a need to explore everything with him, but feared telling him that. What if he wanted more than a mere kiss? "I believe we are." It was a cowardly answer when she wanted more from him.

"I'm glad," he said, then glanced back at the fountain. "I'm going to invite my family to visit. I think it's time. Most of the repairs are finished and we have more furnishings now." He turned toward her. "Is that all right with you?"

She nodded. How could she say no to him? "I'd love to meet them." That was the absolute truth, but a part of her couldn't help being afraid. What if they didn't like her?

He smiled at her, and it filled her with warmth. "They're going to love you. Don't worry overmuch." Samuel leaned down and kissed her cheek. It wasn't on her lips, but it was closer. Perhaps soon he'd do more than offer little comforts.

"You don't know that with any certainty," she said in a shaky tone.

"I do," he said, then brushed a stray lock of hair behind her ear. "Because I know your heart. They'll like you because you are a good person, and you deserve their kindness. Don't diminish yourself. You're worth more than you think you are."

She wanted to believe him, and she would try. "I pray you're right."

"You will see that I am." He stepped away from her. "There are a few things I must see too. Don't stay outside over long. It might rain and I'd hate for you to fall ill." With those words, he walked away from her.

He left much for her to think about. They had an odd sort of relationship, and she didn't quite understand what he wanted from her. She prayed his intentions were good, and in time they might be more than friends. Temperance wanted a true marriage with him. Now all she had to do was discern a way of obtaining it.

CHAPTER 5

December 1629

Samuel's mother and uncle had come to celebrate Christmastide with him and his wife. He had decided to wait to have the rest of his family come to New Berwick. The villagers had welcomed him, but he still didn't quite trust them. His mother had insisted she be allowed to come, and Daniel wouldn't allow her to come on her own. He adored Samuel's mother and would protect her with his life. Their marriage had been necessary, but they had grown to love each other over time.

Much like Samuel had begun to feel for his own wife...

Temperance had been forced to be demure and obedient her entire life. Now that she had the freedom to make her own choices, she'd begun to thrive. Her entire face lit with happiness, and her aura was as bright as sunshine. Samuel didn't want to do anything that might make her revert to her former self. What if he told her how he felt and she rejected him?

He couldn't think of that.

If Temperance didn't love him, he would respect that. He hadn't married her because he loved her, and he wouldn't force her to do something she didn't feel comfortable with.

They were friends, and that would have to be enough. Before he had found out, he would have to marry to regain his land and title, he hadn't wanted a wife or family. He could be content having a companionship with her.

"Why are ye brooding?" Daniel asked.

Samuel glanced up and met his uncle's gaze. "I'm not."

"Dinna think ye are fooling me," he chastised. "I raised ye and I know when ye are wallowing in yer own misery. Tell me what is bothering ye."

He ran his fingers through his hair. Should he explain it to Daniel?

He might have some excellent advice regarding Temperance. Samuel didn't know how to explain his frustration. His wife's aura had changed gradually as she'd grown more comfortable with him, but that didn't mean she wanted to be a real wife. She did care for him, and that shown through; however, there were different versions of love. He couldn't be certain if she loved him in the same way he did her.

"I don't know where to begin." He sighed. "This journey to regain my title took me in a direction I did not expect."

"With yer wife, ye mean," he said in a solemn tone.

Samuel should have realized Daniel would go right to the heart of the matter. He had never been able to hide anything from his uncle. Daniel didn't need any gifts or abilities to read a situation. He had a keen insight all his own. "Yes," he admitted. "I never expected..."

"Tae love her?" Daniel finished for him. "Love is no something one can plan fer. Ye either feel it or ye never do. It's a gift one should never dismiss, at least no lightly."

"I know." He closed his eyes and took a deep breath. Samuel had nothing else to say to that. Daniel spoke the absolute truth. "She's important to me."

"Have ye told her that?" Daniel said in a quiet tone.

He shook his head. "I didn't wish to frighten her." He met his uncle's gaze. "Her father isn't a good man. He mistreated her, and it left deep emotional scars. I've been giving her space to find herself and what she wants."

Daniel was quiet for several moments. "That was

wise of ye." His lips curved into a smile. "Yer mother likes her. They have been spending a lot of time together."

"I have noticed." His wife seemed to prefer his mother's company to his. Samuel didn't blame Temperance. Ailis Noble had a gentle but fierce soul. She protected those she cared about, and she had come to care for Samuel's wife in the short time they had been acquainted. "I'm glad. Temperance doesn't have many people she can rely upon. My mother will be good for her. She never knew her own mother."

"As ye never knew yer father." Daniel nodded. "She probably understands yer pain, as ye do hers. This also is good."

"It has helped us," Samuel agreed. "But that isn't enough to build a marriage on."

"Yer right in that, but dinna ye think ye have more than that?" Daniel lifted a brow. "Ye have love and respect even if ye haven't admitted that to each other. It is time that ye told her how ye feel. Take a leap of faith, lad, and ye will be rewarded for yer efforts."

Samuel wanted to believe that, he did. He took risks every day of his life, but somehow this one seemed inherently more precarious. His heart had never been so full of love and anxiety. Telling Temperance he loved her would be the biggest risk he'd ever undertaken. She alone had the ability to break him, as no one ever had. If she turned away from him, he might never fully recover from her rejection. He took a deep breath. "What if she doesn't love me?"

"Then at least ye will no the truth of it." His uncle placed his hand on Samuel's shoulder. "Isn't it better tae know how she feels instead of all the worrying and wondering? Once ye have her answer, ye can move forward. Staying in the same place all yer life is no a good place to reside. Change can be a wondrous thing."

Samuel nodded. "Then I'll take a chance that she loves me." He had to stop being afraid of rejection and finally tell her how he felt. Love was a good thing, and even if she did not feel the same way, he didn't regret loving her. Opening his heart to others had always been difficult for him. She'd opened him up to new possibilities, and he hoped that as they spent their life together they would each continue to grow.

"Good fer ye," Daniel said. "Now go find yer wife and declare your love."

He nodded at his uncle, but did not say another word. Instead, he left his uncle's side and went in search of his wife.

TEMPERANCE HAD BEEN ANXIOUS EVER SINCE SAMUEL told her he was inviting his family to come stay with them. It hadn't taken long to realize she'd been apprehensive for no reason. Ailis had embraced her immediately and treated her like part of her family. It was something Temperance had never felt before, and at first she hadn't known how to handle her acceptance.

Samuel had been acting strangely, too. He kept staring at her as if he expected something from her, but she didn't know what he wanted. She knew what she would like from him, but he hadn't come forth to claim her as his wife, and Temperance was starting to believe he never would.

"Temperance," Samuel called to her.

She turned to meet his gaze. He seemed anxious, but what could make him feel that way? "What is it?" she asked in a concerned tone.

"There is something I wish to speak to you about." He pulled her hand into his. "Can you join me in my study?"

What could he possibly have to say to her? Her heart started to beat heavily. He was usually so calm and it comforted her that he could be so steadfast. For him to be the one distressed by something unnerved her. "Of course," she readily agreed.

He kept her hand in his as they walked down the corridor to his study. Samuel remained silent the entire trek there. His silence proved to make her emotions spike with each step they took. They went inside his study, and he shut the door with a soft click.

"Come sit down," he said. She settled onto the settee, and he joined her there. "There has been something I have wished to discuss with you for a while, but first I have something for you." He reached over and pulled a small box off a nearby table. "I want you to have this."

She took the box from him and opened it. Inside nestled on black velvet, was a broach. It was a flower of delicate gold with three intricately crafted petals. In the center was a sapphire stone that shimmered in the candlelight, and along the stem nestled five tiny diamonds. It was gorgeous. Temperance glanced up at him. "Why do you want me to have this?"

He smiled. "My father gave it to my mother when they married. It was his wedding gift to her, and one of the few items my mother was able to save when she fled Scotland before my birth. She gave it to me years ago to give to my bride on our wedding day."

He took the broach out of the box and pinned it to her dress. "I never planned to marry. The reasons my family fled were not completely a lie."

"I do not understand." Were they really witches? Was that what he was trying to tell her?

Samuel frowned. "We do not worship evil. My family believes in God and attends church like any other person here." He closed his eyes and took a deep breath. "I am not trying to frighten you. There are things you need to understand and I think I can trust you with the truth."

"You can," she insisted. Temperance wanted to be a part of his family. Whatever his truth turned out to be. She loved him. "Tell me everything."

"My father, and my two aunts were convicted as witches and burned on a pyre," he began. "That part, you know. What you do not know is that they had gifts. What some of us have considered a curse."

She swallowed a lump in her throat. "What are these gifts?"

He met her gaze. "Aunt Caitriona had visions, Aunt Sorcha could experience other's feelings—an empath, and my father..." He paused a moment and looked away from her. "He saw colors...the truth of a person can be seen in their aura." Samuel turned to her. "It isn't infallible, but it helps discern a person's intentions. My father passed his gift to me."

She stared at him, startled by his admission. "What can you see in me?"

Samuel smiled. "Kindness, honesty, and loyalty." He cupped her cheek in his hand. "I know that I can rely on your discretion and that you would never willingly harm anyone."

He couldn't see how much she loved him... "Why are you telling me this now?"

"Because I love you, and I do not believe a husband and wife should have any secrets from each other." He leaned closer to her. "I never wanted to marry, but in my dismissal of marriage, I never imagined I could have a wife like you. Every day I'm surprised by my love for you and I do not want to live another day without having a true marriage. I'm done denying what I feel" He ran his thumb across her lips. "Will you have me knowing my curse?"

"You're not cursed," she told him. Her love for him grew more fierce with every breath she took. "You're blessed. What happened to your father and aunts is a tragedy, but do not allow their misfortune to guide your entire life." She pressed her lips to his in a quick kiss. "I love you too, and I do not want this distance between us."

"Thank heaven," he said, then pulled her into his arms. He pressed his lips to hers in a more passionate kiss. When she opened her mouth on a sigh of pleasure, he deepened the kiss. His tongue touched hers, delicately at first, then with unyielding desire.

Temperance moaned and wrapped her arms around his neck. His kisses grew more fervent with each pass of his lips over hers, and she relished the passion between them.

Samuel pulled back. "This is not the place to explore our need for each other. My mother expects us for the evening meal shortly." His breathing was heavy. "We can celebrate tonight, and for the rest of our lives the love we share."

"Yes," she said in a hoarse tone. Temperance

hadn't believed she could be loved or find happiness. Her marriage was a gift she never expected to have. She adored Samuel and would always be thankful fate had brought him into her life. Samuel's love enchanted her, and she fully intended to enjoy living happily-ever-after by his side.

Ten years later...

Samuel stared out into the garden. His mother was out there near the fountain. Temperance chased their twin daughters and son around the fountain, while Samuel's mother smiled at their antics. Honor Caitriona and Patience Sorcha had their mother's dark hair and silver-colored eyes, and their son was a mini replica of him. They twins were born a year after they decided to have a real marriage.

No more children had been born to them for three years after the twins came into their lives. Samuel had accepted that the twins would be his only children. He found it ironic that everyone had been so concerned he had a son to pass his title to, and he'd been blessed with two daughters. He adored Honor and Patience.

But then, by some sort of miracle, Temperance had become pregnant again before the twins' fourth birthday. When his son had been born, he'd cried. Not because he had been hoping for a son, but because his heart was bursting with love. Why had he ever believed he shouldn't have this? His family was the greatest gift he'd ever been given, and he would lay down his life to keep them.

They named their son Niall Daniel after the two most important men in Samuel's life.

After the tumultuous start to Samuel's life it seemed fitting that he was back where he belonged with a wife he adored beyond all reason, and children that filled his heart to near bursting with love. He didn't believe in fairy tales or happy endings, but fate had given him a version of one.

"Samuel," his mother called to him. "Come join us."

He shook his head. He'd hug and kiss them all later. For now, this was all he wanted. To bask in his joy and their laughter.

His mother chuckled, but nodded at him. She understood more than most what they had lost. The villagers had accepted him back into their lives, and he would do his best to ensure they never had cause to persecute his family again.

So far his children showed no signs they had any of the three gifts, but he and Temperance were ever vigilant. Should the children have one of the gifts they would need to be counseled on their usage. He would not lose his children to the bigotry he'd lost his father and aunts to.

The children swarmed his mother and hugged her. Temperance slipped away from them and came to his side. Samuel pulled her into his arms and kissed her lips. A quick affectionate kiss, one that had come naturally for him to give her, even in the presence of his family. "I love you," he whispered into her ear.

"And I love you," she said. Her smile was bright, and her happiness glowed around her.

Life was a journey of unexpected joy and hardships. Both Samuel and Temperance had their fair share, but at least now they had each other to see them through it. She leaned her head on his shoulder, and he held her close to him.

Sometimes you get exactly what you wished for, and other times you receive something you never knew you wanted. He had been worn, jaded, and bitter from what had been taken from his family. He hadn't wanted to love anyone. It hurt too much to allow someone into his life. Until Temperance... She'd changed his beliefs on love and family.

Temperance had slipped into his heart seamlessly, and she fit there perfectly. She'd enchanted him, and with her he could believe in forever—he did believe in forever. She was his everything.

ABOUT DAWN BROWER

USA TODAY Bestselling author, DAWN BROWER writes both historical and contemporary romance. There are always stories inside her head; she just never thought she could make them come to life. That creativity has finally found an outlet.

Growing up she was the only girl out of six children. She is a single mother of two teenage boys; there is never a dull moment in her life. Reading books is her favorite hobby and she loves all genres.

HISTORICAL

Stand alone:

Broken Pearl

A Wallflower's Christmas Kiss

A Gypsy's Christmas Kiss

Marsden Romances

A Flawed Jewel

A Crystal Angel

A Treasured Lily

A Sanguine Gem

A Hidden Ruby

A Discarded Pearl

Marsden Descendants

Rebellious Angel

Tempting An American Princess

How to Kiss a Debutante

Loving an America Spy

Linked Across Time

Saved by My Blackguard

Searching for My Rogue

Seduction of My Rake

Surrendering to My Spy

Spellbound by My Charmer

Stolen by My Knave

Separated from My Love

Scheming with My Duke

Secluded with My Hellion

Secrets of My Beloved

Spying on My Scoundrel

Shocked by My Vixen

Smitten with My Christmas Minx

Vision of Love

Enduring Legacy

The Legacy's Origin

Charming Her Rogue

Ever Beloved

Forever My Earl

Always My Viscount

Infinitely My Marquess

Eternally My Duke

Bluestockings Defying Rogues

When An Earl Turns Wicked

A Lady Hoyden's Secret

One Wicked Kiss

Earl In Trouble

All the Ladies Love Coventry

One Less Scandalous Earl

Confessions of a Hellion

The Vixen in Red

Lady Pear's Duke

Scandal Meets Love

Love Only Me (Amanda Mariel)

Find Me Love (Dawn Brower)

If It's Love (Amanda Mariel)

Odds of Love (Dawn Brower)

Believe In Love (Amanda Mariel)

Chance of Love (Dawn Brower)

Love and Holly (Amanda Mariel)

Love and Mistletoe (Dawn Brower

The Neverhartts

Never Defy a Vixen

Never Disregard a Wallflower

Never Dare a Hellion

Never Deceive a Bluestocking

Never Disrespect a Governess

Never Desire a Duke

CONTEMPORARY

Stand alone:

Deadly Benevolence

Snowflake Kisses

Kindred Lies

Sparkle City

Diamonds Don't Cry

Hooking a Firefly

Novak Springs

Cowgirl Fever

Dirty Proof

Unbridled Pursuit

Sensual Games

Christmas Temptation

Daring Love

Passion and Lies

Desire and Jealousy

Seduction and Betrayal

Begin Again

There You'll Be

Better as a Memory

Won't Let Go

Heart's Intent

One Heart to Give

Unveiled Hearts

Heart of the Moment

Kiss My Heart Goodbye

Heart in Waiting

Heart Lessons

A Heart Redeemed

Kismet Bay

Once Upon a Christmas

New Year Revelation

All Things Valentine

Luck At First Sight

Endless Summer Days

A Witch's Charm

All Out of Gratitude

Christmas Ever After

YOUNG ADULT FANTASY

Broken Curses

The Enchanted Princess

The Bespelled Knight

The Magical Hunt

ABOUT AMANDA MARIEL

USA Today Bestselling, Amazon All Star author Amanda Mariel dreams of days gone by when life moved at a slower pace. She enjoys taking pen to paper and exploring historical time periods through her imagination and the written word. When she is not writing she can be found reading, crocheting, traveling, practicing her photography skills, or spending time with her family.

Visit www.amandamariel.com for more information on Amanda and her books. Sign up for her newsletter while you are on her site and receive a free ebook!

Love Only Me

Find Me Love

If it's Love

Odd's of Love

Believe in Love

Chance of Love

Love and Holly

Love and Mistletoe

A Rogue's Kiss Series

Her Perfect Rogue

His Perfect Hellion

Coming next to the A Rogue's Kiss series

Her Perfect Scoundrel

Standalone titles

One Moonlit Tryst

One Enchanting Kiss

Christmas in the Duke's Embrace

One Wicked Christmas

A Lyon in Her Bed (The Lyon's Den connected world)

Courting Temptation (House of Devon connected world)

Wicked Earls' Club

Titles by Amanda Mariel

Earl of Grayson

Earl of Edgemore

Earl of Persuasion

Fated for a Rogue

A Wallflower's Folly

One Fateful May Day

Fate Gave Me a Duke

Coming next to the Fated for a Rogue series

Fated for Folly

Connected by a Kiss

These are designed so they can standalone

How to Kiss a Rogue (Amanda Mariel)

A Kiss at Christmastide (Christina McKnight)

A Wallflower's Christmas Kiss (Dawn Brower)

Stealing a Rogue's Kiss (Amanda Mariel)

A Gypsy's Christmas kiss (Dawn Brower)

A Duke's Christmas Kiss (Tammy Andresen)

Box sets and anthologies

Visit www.amandamariel.com to see Amanda's current offerings.

ONE ENCHANTING KISS

AMANDA MARIEL

ONE ENCHANTING KISS

PROLOGUE

France, 1605

Moire smiled at Ma and Lili as she kneaded a ball of bread dough. The pair stood across the counter from her working their own batches of the pliant mixture. A streak of flour coated Lili's cheek, while Ma's apron bore her handprints. Moire imagined she too must look a fright for when the baking was finished, she always did. "How many loaves are we to make this day?"

"Nae too many. Six ought to do." Ma flipped her dough, then began kneading it once more. "We've four loaves ordered. Two for the manor house, and one each for the inn and Mrs. Moreau. 'Tis good to keep a couple extras at the ready."

The kitchen's heat caused sweat to bead on Moire's forehead, but she didn't dare wipe it away. She blew out a breath as she continued working the dough, then glanced out the window. The sun was high in the sky, shining brightly on the village.

"You should not complain, Moire." Lili brushed a stray curl from her forehead leaving a fresh streak of white powder in her wake. "'Tis lucky we are that so many of the villagers purchase our baked goods."

"I wasn't complaining." Moire peered at her twin. "Simply asking a question."

France had been good to her—to all of them. They'd built a pleasant home and a sustainable living here in the years since they'd fled Scotland. Da had his blacksmith shop and Aunt Ailis, who had become their mama years ago, supplemented the family's coin by selling her breads and pastries.

Furthermore, the villagers had been kind and accepting when Moire's family settled here. Over the years, many had become their friends. She'd even begun a courtship with one of the town's gentlemen. Bastien Roux had started calling on Moire a week prior, and she found herself rather taken with the handsome young man.

Of course she was not in love, but believed with time the emotion could develop between them. A ghost of a smile turned her lips up at the thought. "In fact, I feel blessed."

Moire set the loaf she'd been working on aside and scowled at Lili as she reached for more flour. "I hope never to leave France."

"Indeed." Lili's expression faltered, her cheery disposition turning sour for a heartbeat. "Forget I said anything."

Moire grinned, satisfaction swelling within her. But trepidation followed in its wake. The way Lili faltered reminded her that not all was well.

Lili had been on edge of late, claiming to feel anxiety and fear creeping into the village, and she'd not deny her own visions had increased. Likewise the girls brothers, Samuel and Lachlan had been experiencing anxious reservations.

Lachlan never spoke much about his abilities, though he'd been even more reserved of late, which did not sit well with Moire. Samuel was the most concerning of the lot. He insisted the family should leave France, but failed to give any reason for his adamant requests.

How she wished she knew what was afoot.

She'd had three visions in the past sennight, but nothing that made sense. The first two were quick flashes of women she did not know in places she'd never seen. The most recent vision showed her neighbor woman. It was a tad more powerful and lasted a bit longer, but still made little sense to her.

It was Moire's neighbor, the widow Pierre,

crouched in a dark corner weeping and pleading with someone. "No, please. You have it wrong. Please," she'd begged. Then the vision faded away as quickly as it had come on. Moire exhaled a slow breath, pushing away the uneasy feeling threatening to steal her breath.

"What's the matter, Moire?" Lili dusted the flour from her hands as she pinned Moire beneath her sympathetic stare. "Do not try to hide it. I feel yer upset and I ken it's naught to do with our disagreement."

Moire wasn't the least bit surprised, for it was Lili's gift to feel others emotions. She'd worked hard to suppress her worry and fear these past days in order to keep from alarming Lili, as well as Lachlan. There was nothing for it now. She'd have to be forthright. "I've been having visions."

Ma leaned closer across the counter, worry etched in the fine lines of her face. "Ye must tell us what ye've seen, lass."

"I am afraid there's not much to tell. They have been more like quick flashes that do not reveal anything, but leave me with the feeling something bad is afoot." Moire glanced toward the entrance of their cottage at the sound of the door creaking. "Da, ye are home…early."

Her stomach sank when Samuel and Lachlan strolled in behind him. The boys were born her cousins but had long since become her brothers.

Both possessed their own special gift—or gifts, in Lachlan's case, for he had all three. Samuel had the ability to see people's colors—understand the intentions of their souls.

Da strolled into the kitchen as Samuel closed the cottage's heavy wooden door. "Lachlan had a vision."

"As did Moire." Ma embraced Da, and he dropped a kiss on the top of her head. "She was just now telling Lili and me about it."

"What did you see?" Lachlan and Moire asked one another in unison, their voices echoing through the small room.

A trickle of dread washed through Moire. "You first," she said, then dropped into a chair, exhaustion taking hold of her. Between the heat and her frayed nerves, she'd had more than enough for one day.

Still, she needed to know what Lachlan had seen. Propping her fist under her chin, she turned her attention to him.

A shrill scream permeated the room before he could speak, and Moire sprang to her feet. "What the devil?" She followed Da and Lachlan to the window where Ma, Samuel, and Lili quickly joined them.

"So much fear," Lili whispered, her voice shaking.

Moire inhaled a deep breath, her gaze pinned to the scene unfolding outside. Her throat tightened in horror. Hands shaking, she braced herself against the window ledge.

Two men had hold of the Widow Pierre and were

dragging her kicking and screaming from her home. Moire swallowed hard, wishing to look away but at the same time unable to stop watching. She wanted to run into the street. To help the poor old woman. Demand the men release her. But all she could manage to do was stare.

Samuel said, "And anger…their auras are burning red."

Lili turned away, covering her face with her hands. "She's so afraid…so upset. Why are they taking her?"

"She's innocent…" Lachlan shook his head.

Da wrapped his arm around Lili. "Come now, lassie." He guided her to a chair and helped her to sit before turning to the others. "Lachlan, ye'd best be telling everyone what you saw now."

Samuel tugged on Da's arm. "We should pack what we can and leave first. He can tell the lasses as we travel."

Ma wrapped her arms around Samuel and pulled him close. "Hush now."

Moire turned her full attention to Lachlan and nibbled her lower lip as she waited for him to speak. She'd wager his vision matched her own. Perhaps he'd envisioned the missing piece that would make what she'd seen make sense.

He glanced at the ceiling, releasing a slow breath. "I saw that." He pointed at the window. "Widow Pierre being accused of witchcraft and dragged away." He balled his fists at his sides. "She's nae a witch. Just a lonely old woman."

Moire swallowed past the lump in her throat. "I saw her too. In a dark, dirty place. She was scared and pleading with someone."

Da's strong hand came to rest on Moire's shoulder and she leaned her head against his arm.

Lachlan shook his head. "I'm afraid Samuel is right. We canna stay here much longer."

Moire's heart sank. She had no wish to leave France—to leave Bastien. She picked up her head, standing tall. "Why ever not? This is our home."

"We are more at risk than anyone else here." Lachlan gave her a knowing stare.

"Nae, we've been careful." Moire straightened her back and notched her chin. "No one kens our secret."

"I saw Lili being dragged away in chains. Fire set to our cottage. Ma cryin'." Lachlan shook his head. "We must go before my vision can come to pass." He stared at Moire. "Ye ken as well as I that the only way tae stop it is tae change course."

"Me? But why?" Lili's voice whispered through the room.

Da looked to Ma. "I think the time tae be telling them what happened in Scotland has come."

Ma gave a firm nod. "Everyone sit."

Moire exhaled an exasperated breath as her family settled into place around the old wood table. "We already ken about Scotland."

A tear slid from Da's eye as he shook his head. "Nae, not the full of it, Lass."

"You see," Ma paused, taking Da's hand in hers, "we did nae leave Scotland because we wished tae. We fled in order tae protect ye as well as ourselves."

"From what?" Lili turned wide eyes on Da.

He brushed the stray tear from his cheek. "Yer Ma, God rest her soul, along with Samuel's Da and Lachlan's Ma, were accused of being witches." His voice cracked with emotion and Lili rested her hand on his arm, rubbing small circles. "Yer dear Ma told me tae protect the wee ones," he said as he glanced at the woman she now called Ma, "and yer Aunt Ailis."

Ma frowned, her eyes glistening with unshed tears. "People did not understand their gifts any more than they would yers. Its why we taught ye tae keep them hidden. I do not ken how we'd be discovered, but Lachlan and Samuel are right. We must go."

Lachlan's chair scraped the floor as he repositioned himself. "What of my Da?"

"It's all too sad." Ma hung her head, her shoulders quivering. "The mob that came after yer Ma hit yer Da so hard he never had a chance." Sniffling, Ma raised her head to meet Lachlan's gaze. "Perhaps it was a blessin', for he escaped the torch."

Moire's heart thundered. Her ma had been burned—accused of being a witch… Murdered.

She wanted to scream, to run, to forget all she'd been told. She'd known her Ma died along with the others, but she'd always been told it was an accident. Nothing more. She clenched her hands in her lap and stared at Da. "And now the same fate is to befall us?"

"Nae." Samuel stood. "No one has come yet. We must leave before they do."

Ma nodded as she rose to her feet. "Quickly now. Take only what ye must, and nothin' more than ye can carry."

Lili stopped halfway across the kitchen, turning back toward their parents. "Where are we tae go? Spain as the others have?"

"Nae," Da shook his head, "We will travel tae the coast by foot, then board a ship for England."

"Now hurry." Ma waved her hands toward the kitchen door.

Moire raced after Lili, entering their bedchamber directly behind her. Neither wasted time talking as they stuffed what they needed into valises. Her task complete, Moire stood near the door watching Lili. Her sweet sister shook from head to toe as she packed her bag. Was this to be the way of things for the rest of their lives? Always hiding their gifts? Waiting for the day they would have to leave everything behind again? What of their future children?

Moire closed her eyes against the thoughts and emotions sweeping through her. There were many things she could not control, but she made her mind up in that instant. God as her witness, she would control the things she could.

She'd make sure not to pass on her gift, ensure that her children would not share her worries. Moire would never marry. Never have a family of her own.

"Moire."

She opened her eyes to find Lili standing beside her, valise in hand. "Are ye ready?" Moire asked.

Lili nodded and moved past her, then pivoted to face her and stopped. "What were ye thinking about a moment ago."

"That I will never marry." Moire said.

Lili tilted her head ever so slightly. "But of course ye will."

"Nae, I will not. For I refuse to bring children into such a cruel world." Moire squared her shoulders, notched her chin. "I will not subject an innocent bairn tae any of this." She waved her hand at the space around them. "Not have them worry over their safety, or mine."

Lili stared at her, sympathy filling her crystal blue eyes. "I understand, though I hope ye reconsider someday."

"I shan't. Not ever." Moire shook her head firmly. "Tis not a gift we have. "Tis a curse."

Lili sighed. "Yer wrong, and someday ye'll ken it."

Moire shook her head as she followed Lili out of the room. She didn't ken what life would be like minutes from now, but she was determined to follow her own course. She'd lead a solitary life. That of a spinster—alone and unable to pass along her curse. She'd not have blood on her hands.

Nothing would persuade her otherwise.

London, 1610

The hot summer sun beat down on Moire as she made her way through the crowded London streets. All around her she could hear the calls of street peddlers, the shuffling of skirts and feet, the pounding of hooves, and the creaking of carriage wheels, but she didn't dare make eye contact with anyone.

Her sweaty palms were making it hard for her to maintain a grip on her basket as she continued down the street. She wiped her palm on her skirt, then shuffled the basket into her dry hand before wiping the other. Most of the time Moire stayed within the safety of her home. She hated the risk of going out—the constant fear of discovery.

When Ma insisted Moire make a delivery of their baked goods, she did her best to see the task completed quickly. Moire did not chat with anyone, nor did she make eye contact when it could be avoided. She wasn't rude, she simply did not make unnecessary efforts to be friendly. The risk was far too great that someone would discover her secret—and if her past had taught her anything, it was just how deadly her gift could be.

Relief swept through her as she opened the door to her home and stepped inside. Here she needn't worry overmuch. Her siblings had special gifts as well, and her parents always protected them. They'd been taught to hide their abilities from the outside world, but never to be afraid or ashamed of them. She was free to be herself inside of these walls—free to breathe easy around her family.

Moire strolled into the kitchen and set her basket down. Her gaze caught Lili's, and the joy radiating from her sister caused Moire to smile. "Ye look overjoyed, sister."

"I am nearly bursting with it." Lili's grin widened.

Ma dusted her hands on her apron. "'Tis a happy day indeed."

"What have I missed?" Moire asked.

Lili cast a glance at Ma before turning back to Moire. "William has asked for my hand." Her smile widened as she continued, "and I've accepted. We're tae be wed." She beamed, scooping Moire's hands into hers. "Isna wonderful news. I'm tae be Mrs. William North."

Moire's throat threatened to close as she uttered, "Wonderful."

In truth, it was disastrous news. Not that she begrudged her sister happiness, love, or a family of her own, but this meant that another—a person outside of their family—would learn their secret. What if Mr. North could not be trusted? Beads of sweat broke out on Moire's forehead and her hands began to shake.

"The color has drained from yer face." Ma gave her a glass of water then steered her toward a chair. "Sit."

"She's afraid," Lili said, "I can feel the fear radiatin' from her." She sat next to Moire and turned sympathetic eyes on her. "Dinna be. William is a kind and understandin' man. He kens I feel deeply and says I am all the more special for it. Oh, please, do be happy for us."

Moire took a drink of the cool water. She wanted to be supportive, to celebrate her sister's joy, but could not shake her growing trepidation. Accepting Lili's gift only meant that he loved her, but did his feelings run deeply enough to shield them all?

"Have ye reason to react as ye are?" Ma asked, worry in her sky-blue gaze.

"Nae." Moire shook her head. "'Tis only my own worry over our safety."

"Ye needn't fret. Mr. North comes from a good family. He's honorable, trustworthy, and in love with our Lili. He'd not be doin' anything to harm her," Ma said.

"I ken that."

Lili sighed. "Then be happy for me."

Moire ignored the pounding of her heart, the memories of all that had happened to her family because of their secret, and forced a small grin. "I am, Lili. Truly, I am. 'Tis only my fear of discovery dampenin' my joy."

Moire had spent much of her life hiding her gift and resenting its very existence. On more than one occasion, the special abilities of her family had caused them grief. First when her Mother, aunt, and uncle were accused of being witches and burned at the stake. Then again when the family had been forced to flee from France to London. Where would they go if trouble found them again?

Would they be able to escape the fate dealt to their Mother and her siblings? Perhaps the day would come when there'd be nowhere new to run to. They would be cornered. Moire drew in a shaky breath, willing herself to calm down.

She had worked too hard to hide—not only her ability to see the past and future, but also herself—to be found out now. All Moire wished for was a quiet and safe existence. She wanted as much for her whole family, but she must find a way to accept that Lili wished for more. Come what may, Moire had to support her sister.

"Ye mustn't allow fear tae rule ye, lass." Ma patted her shoulder. "Open yer heart, allow others in. Ye deserve happiness too. Yer Ma would have wanted as much for ye."

Moire nodded her head as if she agreed, but in truth she knew she would never follow the well-meaning advice. She'd vowed never to wed and held as steadfast to her oath today as she did when she'd made the vow. "Let's not dwell on me. Ye'll make a bonny bride, Lili. When is the ceremony tae take place?"

Lili's blue gaze sparkled with merriment as she stared at Moire. "We're tae have an engagement party tomorrow, then once the banns have been read, we'll marry in the church. We do not wish to wait overlong."

Moire smiled at Lili then turned to Ma. "She'll be needin' a new dress."

"Aye." Ma agreed. "Once we've finished our bakin' we'll begin workin' on one. I was thinkin' we could refashion her blue dress with bits of lace and pearl."

"I do so love that one." Lili retrieved her apron and tied it around her trim waist. "'Tis all so excitin', I fear I may burst with joy."

"Indeed." Moire joined Ma and Lili at the counter then set to work on a batch of biscuits. She put all of her energy and focus into her baking, ignoring the needling fear that continued to prick at her.

Moire shaped the biscuits and placed them in the oven. How she wished Lachlan was here. He'd be able to either reassure her or convince the others that disaster loomed. He often had visions that she did not, and vice versa. Between the two of them, they rarely missed a thing of importance. Surely if trouble did stand beyond their door, Lachlan would write to warn them.

She would have to let her trepidation go and focus on what was most important—Lili. Moire glanced at her sister and her heart swelled with joy despite the fear assaulting her. Lili truly would make a bonny bride and a fine wife as well. She deserved a loving husband and children—they all did. Nonetheless, 'twas a risk Moire would never allow herself to take.

She chased all thoughts from her mind and focused on her work as Ma and Lili chatted about the impending wedding and all that must be done.

By the time Da and Samuel returned home from the blacksmith shop, Moire's fingers hurt from kneading and shaping the dough. They had baked everything from bread to pies in preparation for the engagement party.

Ma moved to the wash basin and untied her apron. "Let us clean up and greet yer Da."

Moire wiped her sticky hands, then piled biscuits into a wicker basket while Lili removed the last loaf of bread from the oven.

"There's my lasses." Da strolled into the kitchen and set a bundle wrapped in brown paper on the table. "'Tis for ye, Lili."

He wrapped Ma in his arms and dropped a kiss on her lips, then looked back at Lili. "Open it, lass, what are ye waiting for?"

Moire studied Lili as she carefully unwrapped the bundle, revealing a pile of blue and cream damask shot through with silver threads. Lili stroked her fingers across the material before smiling at Da. "'Tis beautiful."

"We canna send ye to yer husband in rags, now can we?" Da winked.

"None of us wears rags." Ma playfully swatted his arm and Da chuckled.

Moire came up next to Lili and lifted the fabric off the table to hold it by Lili's chest. "Look at how it matches her eyes. Ye'll be the most stunning bride there ever was by the time we're done with ye."

Da grinned. "Aye, she will. Our little Lili is all grown up."

Ma pulled away from Da and wrapped her arms around Moire and Lili. "Indeed. Both of our bonny lasses have grown into fine women. Now let us get to work on Lili's gown. We haven't much time."

Moire's panic resurfaced as Ma led her and Lili from the kitchen. How the devil was she to get through the engagement party, or the wedding for that matter, when she could not manage to push her worry aside while in the safety of her home?

Lili squeezed her hand and whispered, "Have faith, all will be well."

Moire squeezed back, hoping with all she had that Lili was right.

Thank you so much for taking the time to read *One Enchanting Kiss*.

Your opinion matters!

Please take a moment to review this book on your favorite review site and share your opinion with fellow readers.

USA Today bestselling author

~Heartwarming historical romances that leave you breathless~

CHARMING HER ROGUE
ENDURING LEGACY 10

A LINKED ACROSS TIME NOVEL

DAWN BROWER

ENDURING
LEGACY

CHARMING HER ROGUE

June 18, 1914

*L*ady Catherine Langdon twirled the champagne in her glass, staring at the bubbles as they popped against the side of the crystal. Music echoed throughout the room as a violinist strummed out Vivaldi's *The Four Seasons*. Catherine would have preferred something a little more soothing to ease her current distress, but she didn't have much say for anything in her life. She considered herself a modern woman, yet she had to continue to follow the dictates of society.

At one and twenty, she'd have liked to have found her own residence and used her inheritance as she saw fit. That wasn't to be her fate though. Her father had ensured she had a guardian for all things, and she wouldn't have control of her funds for four more years. If she married, they'd go to her husband. Catherine didn't have any intention of allowing something so archaic to happen to her. No man would ever have power over her.

"Do you find these dinners dreary too?" a male asked from behind her.

She'd been so caught up in her own thoughts that she'd failed to notice his presence until he'd spoken. Catherine turned to glance up at him. He was tall and foreboding. Some ladies might be intimidated by that, but not Catherine. He had golden blond hair with highlights streaked throughout that suggested he spent time outdoors in full sunlight. One strand fell loose over his forehead in an enticing curl. His eyes were like shiny emeralds that mesmerized her for a few brief moments until she regained her composure.

"They can be rather tedious," she confirmed. "But they appear to be a necessity for the ambassador." Sir Benjamin Villiers, her guardian, worked as secretary to the ambassador. Catherine had been living in France with him since her father's death over a year ago. Some ladies would have been excited to live in Paris and have access to the latest fashions, but not her—never her. Catherine's dark hair came from her father, the former Duke of Thornly, but her sapphire blue eyes were from her mother. Her father's title had passed on to a cousin she'd been barely acquainted with. Her mother had died in childbirth

—after one of the several times she tried to give the duke an heir he desperately needed—or more apt— wanted. Unfortunately, neither her mother nor the child survived. She was completely alone in the world, and sometimes that was more than she could bear.

She wanted so much more than pretty gowns and shiny baubles. They were nice, and she did appreciate not having to worry about money. Some things were far more important though. She'd been secretly studying to become a nurse. Sir Benjamin would be appalled if he found out. She prayed he continued to remain ignorant of her pastime. With the current climate of the political world, she feared such skills might prove necessary—though she prayed her instincts proved wrong.

Certain gifts had been bestowed upon members of her family that dated back centuries. Some of her ancestors had been persecuted as witches. Her mother was a direct descendant of that line, and now her. Catherine's name came from a variation of one of those long-ago witches—Caitrìona. Catherine even had the same gift as the woman who'd been presumed wicked and a servant of the devil. Those who didn't understand their abilities chose to believe the people who had them were immoral, but her family considered their abilities a blessing from someplace good.

The thing about gifts—sometimes they came in

threes. She'd been somehow blessed with all of the abilities, but one remained stronger than the rest. Her premonitions didn't come in flashes, but more like feelings emphasized by the emotions of people around her. Her strongest and most reliable ability centered around that amplification, and sometimes she had trouble deciphering what it all meant. This man projected one thing loudly —secrets. He was hiding something, and whatever it turned out to be could potentially impact the world.

"Some people need society events to function," he said evenly. "I've never been one to put stock in them. Do you enjoy them?"

"Not particularly," she replied. "As you've stated —they're more tiresome than entertaining. If you don't like them, what brings you to this particular one? The ambassador's guests are generally of the prestigious sort."

She'd met numerous individuals that boasted of their importance. Catherine hadn't found any of them especially noteworthy. She hadn't relied on her gifts for any epiphanies where they were concerned. In her experience, if someone talked that much about themselves, it usually meant they were of little consequence. It was the quiet ones she had to watch and figure out. Like this man—he'd started the conversation, but gave little of himself away.

"It's not my practice to boast about my connec- tions." He reached out and snatched a glass of champagne from a waiter as he strolled past. The man brought it to his lips and sipped the bubbly liquid. Once again, Catherine was transfixed by him, his deeds, and his inaction. Everything about him remained an enigma. What game was he playing? He lowered his glass and met her gaze. "Don't you think it is far better to blend in and not allow anyone to notice you?"

She didn't understand how he'd ever be able to make himself unnoticeable. He was by far the most handsome man in the room, and he oozed charm and arrogance, but perhaps he only showed her that side of himself. He seemed to be a man made up of several facets. He had his charm, the easy-going nature he showed the world, but his eyes had a darkness to them that suggested he had something to hide. But she didn't need to rely completely on suppositions. She'd been born with the ability to see past the façades people used to hide who they truly were. This man had an aura that screamed of secrecy. "I've never been much of a wallflower," she replied. "I enjoy social interaction—most of the time." In fact, she almost needed it.

He tilted his head. "No, you wouldn't be. A woman like you stands out in a crowd. You must have numerous suitors."

"Not particularly," she answered. "At least not here in France. Back home I had a few." None of them made her heart beat faster or her breathing shallow. This man did though. Something about him made her want to move closer, to touch him, and maybe even press her lips to his. To make it simple, he was dangerous to her well-being, and she still didn't even know his name.

"That's a bloody shame." He sipped his sparkling wine again. "I expect you'd be like this champagne. Sweet, tantalizing, and overflowing with pleasure after one taste."

He had to be a rogue of the worst sort. Gentleman didn't say such outrageous things to a lady. Did he believe her to be a cyprian hired for the enjoyment of the men at the party? There were not many females in attendance. Such was the nature of political work—women stayed home more often than not. The other ladies there were wives of the diplomats and their employers. Catherine was the sole unattached woman in attendance. Perhaps she was reading too much into his statement.

"Sir, you're too bold." She narrowed her eyes to glare at him. "I insist you apologize."

He lifted a brow. "You're not any of those things I mentioned?" His lips tilted upward into a sinful smile. Damn him and his gorgeous face. "I don't believe it."

"I'm not a lady you can insult without consequences." She was the daughter of a duke, damn it. Catherine lifted her chin and pinned him with her most haughty stare. "Do you not know who I am?"

He chuckled lightly. "I think all of France is aware of your lineage—certainly everyone in England is."

Catherine took a deep breath and prepared for the impending disagreement. This man rubbed her wrong—and right, at the same time. She fervently wished she didn't find him so attractive. Her body almost hummed with joy in his presence. She'd always followed her instincts in the past; however, she believed, with him, she'd best exercise caution. He was able to hide a part of himself from her gifts, and she couldn't trust him because of that. What made him special?

"Then why do you persist in being so discourteous?" For the life of her, she couldn't discern his motivation for being so arrogant and condescending. She was pleasant to everyone, and he made her want to punch someone for the first time in her entire life. "What have I done for you to be this way with me?"

"Not a thing." He shrugged. "You intrigue me, and I thought I'd ascertain your mettle."

"*Ohh...*" If she was a lady inclined to give into temper tantrums, she'd already be stomping her foot and screaming at the top of her lungs. "You're insufferable."

"Thank you." His lips twitched, and amusement fairly danced out of his eyes. "I do pride myself in being able to needle people in the most unexpected ways."

She rolled her eyes. "In that case, consider your goal achieved."

Catherine disliked him. He was the worst sort of man, and she couldn't fathom what she'd found so compelling before. He could go back to hell as far as she was concerned. It would be a happy day if she never came in contact with him ever again. Some handsome devils shouldn't be encouraged, and he was at the top of that list.

"Does one dance at these things?" He glanced around the room. "It seems as if most people are content with talking about inane topics sure to put me to sleep."

"Let me guess," she began. "You consider yourself and everything about you the very epitome of all that is exhilarating in the world." God save her from men who thought the world revolved around them. She didn't need their ilk paying any attention to her.

"Not at all," he replied smoothly. "But I'm not so boring as to engender individuals into a catatonic state." He gestured to a nearby group. "Just look at them all—their very faces allude to placidity— they're practically asleep standing up."

Catherine sighed. "If you're in such a state of ennui why are you still here?" For that matter, why did she continue to converse with him? She was well past the stage of irritation and had entered into complete annoyance. "You could go home, and all would be well in your world, Mr.—"

"Lord," he interrupted her. "I've never been a mere mister."

Of course he was a *lord*. Arrogance such as his came naturally to some, but those of his ilk were weaned on it. No wonder he oozed it as easily as breathing and didn't apologize for it. "Be that as it may…" She silently prayed for patience. "To answer your earlier question, this was never meant to be the dancing sort of gathering. It's a dinner and conversation. If you want more, you should attend the ball later this week. I'm sure a lord such as yourself will have no problem finding a willing dance partner."

"Will you dance with me?" His lips tilted upward into a sinful smile. His arrogance and self-assurance flowed through her in waves. "That is why you suggested I attend the next ball is it not?" He lifted a brow questioningly.

The polite thing would be to say yes. That was what was expected of her, after all… "Absolutely not." She couldn't stop herself from saying it. "I don't believe we'd manage a full set before I wanted to strangle you. It's best to save us both from that disastrous outcome."

Instead of being offended, he grinned widely as if she'd complimented him. He was such a contrary bastard. "I think I like you."

"Please don't," she begged. "I don't need you to be charming. Liking you is the last thing I wish to do."

At the start of their conversation she'd have liked nothing more. Now that she'd spent some time in his company she'd had a change of heart. He might be handsome, and something about him may call out to her, but he was entirely wrong for her. In her experience, it was better to cut all ties in situations such as this one. Catherine didn't need any heartache in her life.

"Ah," He leaned in a little closer. Heat flowed from him to her in waves. "But you do find me fascinating. If it helps, I'm equally charmed by you."

"I assure you that was not my intention." Her cheeks flushed as she warmed from the inside out. She sipped her champagne absentmindedly for lack of any other response to his attention. "Don't take it to heart."

"I fear I already have." He lifted his champagne glass in salute. "But I know when to take a bow. To you, my dear, Lady Catherine." He took a sip after his toast and then winked. "Until we meet again, for I'm sure we will."

With those words, he exited the room. No one noticed, and she wondered briefly if she'd imagined him. No, her premonitions didn't work that way. He'd been real and present. She couldn't help but believe his parting words an omen of sorts—she wished he'd have at least introduced himself. A name would have been nice to know... Catherine fully expected they would cross paths more than once. Somehow, some way, their lives were intertwined. She'd never been wrong before; nonetheless, this was the first time it both terrified and invigorated her all at once.

The flat that Asher Rossington, the Earl of Carrick, had secured for his time in Paris had little to offer. His home in England had a more lavish style to it—but nothing less could be expected from Seabrook. His father—the current Marquess of Seabrook—had thought he needed to explore the world a bit. With limited funds at his disposal, Asher didn't see the point in letting something fancier. All he needed was someplace to sleep in relative peace and comfort.

What his father didn't know was that Asher had been actively engaging in a secret mission with the Earl of Derby—who worked closely with the Under-Secretary of State for War. For whatever reason, the old goat didn't trust his cousin, Sir Benjamin Villiers—who was currently employed by the Ambassador of the United Kingdom to France. The position gave

Sir Benjamin access to a variety of foreign officials. Asher didn't know what he'd done to make his cousin distrust him so, but he didn't see any reason why he couldn't do a little spy work while he was off finding himself. It did run in the family, after all. His great-grandfather—Dominic Rossington, the tenth Marquess of Seabrook, had been a spy during the Napoleonic Wars. He liked the idea of following in his footsteps.

A knock echoed through the room. Asher stared at the door as if it were a foreign substance. Who the hell could possibly be on the other side of it? Sure, opening it would give him the answer to that question, but he had no desire to take the effort. If he ignored it long enough, they'd go away and he could be left in peace. The person knocked again. Asher sighed, then stood and walked over to it. Once he reached it, he yanked it open.

"Telegram monsieur," a boy said and shoved an envelope at him, then left

The front of the envelope was addressed to the Marquess of Seabrook. "Wait, this isn't for me." It couldn't be for him. His father was the marquess. He wouldn't hold that title until… Asher swallowed hard. The only way he'd inherit it was if his father died.

"I deliver them," the boy stopped momentarily and said over his shoulder, "It is up to you what you do with it"

He kept going, not once looking back. Did he not grasp what his delivery meant? His whole life had been turned upside down by one envelope, and he hadn't even broken the seal yet. His father wasn't in France. He should be home at Seabrook—safe and alive. Asher swallowed hard and slowly broke open the envelope. He pulled the missive out, and then fell to his knees. His father... God, he couldn't even think about it. Why had he insisted on Asher having a bloody world tour? The words blurred before him, and he realized why. Tears flowed—he wiped them away furiously, but it didn't help.

He was now the Marquess of Seabrook.

The telegram said his father had died months ago, but they didn't know where to find Asher. So he hadn't even been able to attend his father's funeral. He'd been in Paris for three weeks; before that, he'd been on a boat sailing around Greece, and then he'd taken a train through most of Europe until he decided to work with the Earl of Derby. He'd run into him by chance while in the south of France. Now he was in Paris, facing the fact his father died while he had gallivanted through multiple countries.

He should go home—even if the funeral had been held already. His mother would need his support, and his sisters... They would all be devastated too. Asher couldn't believe his father was gone... Somehow, he managed to crawl back to his feet and set the telegram on a nearby table. At some point, he'd want to re-read it. He should get out of his flat and walk around Paris. Maybe he'd be able to gather his thoughts and make a decision. There was still work he had to do in the city regarding Sir Benjamin. He couldn't say a final goodbye to his father, and going back to England now seemed almost—pointless. Still, he wouldn't make that decision yet.

Asher headed over to the sink to wash away the tears. His insides were torn to shreds, and his emotions jumped all over the place. It would be a while before he could make any rational decisions, and even longer before his grief ebbed. He grabbed a cloth off the shelf and soaked it in warm water, then scrubbed his face—probably longer than necessary, but it soothed him. He wrung it out and set it on the back of the sink, then stared at his reflection in the overhead mirror. His eyes were rimmed red, and his blond hair remained a little damp from the cloth. Hopefully no one noticed how wretched he looked. Hell, he didn't really care if they did, as long as they didn't bother asking what was wrong with him. That one question he didn't want to answer. Partially because he didn't have a clue how.

"Well," he said to himself. "At least I'm not a duke —that would be worse. All those 'Your Graces' would drive me mad." He might be a higher rank, but he was still a lord. Some people might take more notice of him though. A marquess had more pull in the government and society. His father had been a major influence in the House of Lords. That was something Asher would have to consider too. How much did he want to participate in politics?

He walked over and grabbed his jacket. The fresh air would do him good, and it wasn't too hot for June yet. Maybe he'd do the tourist thing. He hadn't had time since he arrived. Truthfully, he was looking for anything to think about other than the news shattering his world. He prayed a distraction of some sort would find its way to him.

LADY CATHERINE STROLLED ALONG THE SIDE OF THE *Pont d'Iéna,* heading toward the Eiffel Tower. She had sneaked out of the embassy to explore the area on her own. Sir Benjamin would have insisted she take someone with her. He believed Paris to be an unsafe place for a young lady. Catherine wanted a little peace and quiet. Strolling along the Seine had seemed like a good idea. Something about the water soothed her soul. She stopped and stared at the river below.

"Don't tell me you're considering something drastic," a male said.

She shook herself out of her reverie and glanced up into *his* green eyes. It had been two days since she'd met him at the embassy. He'd been on her mind ever since. Something she wished she didn't have to admit to—even if it was only to herself. Catherine still didn't know his name, and it irritated her that he hadn't introduced himself. Asking her guardian would have solved the problem; however, it would have caused a new one.

Sir Benjamin would have liked that she'd taken an interest in another male. He did want her to marry and settle down, and something told her he'd have loved it even more when he discovered who she'd been interested in. She might not know his name, but she was certain he had a nice title to go with it. Catherine glared at him. "Depends on what you consider drastic."

"Jumping to your death in the river below."

She stared down at the water and shrugged. "Doesn't seem so bad down there. The jump isn't that high—it's survivable."

He lifted a brow. "You *were* contemplating it."

Taking a swim in the Seine was not high on her list of things to do. There were far better things she could do with her time. She wouldn't explain that to him though. They were barely acquainted, and she owed him nothing. "If I did, would you jump in after me?"

"As a gentleman, I'd be required to," he said almost regrettably. "Please don't make me. I've already had a rather bad day, and I'd be grateful if you didn't make it worse."

"I might consider taking pity on you," she teased.

"For a price." She started to smile, but when she glanced at him, sadness crashed through her. The empathy side of her gift didn't usually come out so harshly. He grieved, and hard… He hadn't been lying when he said he'd had a bad day. What had caused him so much pain?

"Name it," he answered. "I might be willing to pay it." He lifted his lips upward, but there was no happiness there. His eyes even showed a little red around them as if he'd cried. This man had actually shed tears—Catherine couldn't hold the surprise in. Her mouth fell open, yet no words came out. "Cat got your tongue?" The following smirk made her want to wipe it off his face. She'd been feeling sorry for him…

"No," she replied. "Debating what I want."

"A lady such as yourself is bound to be pricy." He winked. "I promise I'm good for it."

He made it sound so suggestive. Catherine's cheeks burned, but she couldn't look away. When she'd left the embassy she never expected her day would involve him. The mystery man whom she wanted to learn more about—the enigma she couldn't solve. "Perhaps there is something you can do for me."

"Oh?" He folded his arms over his chest. "I thought that was the point of this conversation. I'm to pay whatever price you deem acceptable so you don't plunge to your death in the river below." He glanced over the railing. "Please tell me you've reconsidered. I don't wish to get wet today."

She rolled her eyes. "You need not worry. I have no desire to die at the moment." Catherine held out her arm to him. "Will you walk with me?"

He tried to hide it, but the grief hadn't gone away. Every second she spent in his company, that sorrow beat into her. She had to help him, or it would grow. "If you insist," he agreed. "I don't particularly want to return to my flat."

Catherine looped her arm through his. "I hear the Eiffel Tower is nice."

"I wouldn't know," he said. "Never been there."

"It's hard to miss." Catherine laughed lightly and pointed toward it. "It's rather large."

He was quiet and didn't acknowledge what she'd gestured to. Catherine wasn't sure how much more she could take. She had to find a way for him to open up. They would be near the tower soon, and then what? "Are you ever going to introduce yourself to me?"

That made him frown even more. What had she said? Why was his name making him ever sadder than before? They reached the end of the bridge, and he pulled away from her. He turned toward the river and stared at it. "Maybe it was me who wanted to jump and you're the one who saved me."

"It can't be that bad." She reached up and touched his arm. "What is wrong?"

"Life is funny," he began. "You think that you have so much time, but really it's quite finite. Any day could be our last, and yet we continue moving forward."

He'd lost someone. That was why he permeated sorrow. "That's also what makes life beautiful. When you find joy, it should be embraced, and even the hard times teach us something. It gives us a reason to appreciate happiness when we do have it."

Their close proximity made it easier for her to reach into him. This side of her gift didn't always work when she wanted it to. If it did, she might be able to alleviate some of his suffering and make the grief easier to bear. A touch of happiness and a sprinkle of hope—then his outlook would improve. He blinked several times and shook his head. "Did you feel that?"

"What?" Catherine asked innocently. Normally people didn't notice when she helped them with her empathic ability. Maybe she had a bigger connection to this man than she realized. She wasn't sure what it meant, but she'd ponder over all the possibilities later—when she was alone.

"That jolt..." He crinkled his eyebrows together. "You really didn't feel it?"

Catherine could never admit that she'd used anything out of the ordinary to heal him. No one understood her gifts. Her family had been cursed enough by them over the years, and she didn't want him to see her differently. For some reason, she liked him. "I'm afraid I don't know what you're talking about."

He shook his head again. "I suppose it's nothing." His lips tilted upward into a sinful smile. The kind he'd first bestowed upon her at the embassy. He already seemed to be more himself. "You asked if I'd ever introduce myself. Would it be too much for you to call me Ash? I don't like formalities."

"If you insist—Ash," she answered. Why didn't he want her to know who he was? What could he possibly be hiding? He admitted he was a lord already. Since he was aware of her familial relations, surely he must realize that she didn't care about his status amongst the ton. "Then you must call me Cat. All my friends do." Not that she had many, but he didn't need to know that.

"I'm rather glad I ran into you." Ash brushed a stray lock of her hair behind her ear. "I think I needed to find my own Kitty-Cat to make me feel better. Thank you for whatever you did."

"I didn't..." The last thing she'd expected when suggesting he use her nickname was that he'd create one of his own. Catherine wasn't sure how she felt about it either. No one had ever bothered to get that familiar with her before. A part of her liked it, the other part of her was terrified by what it could mean.

"I don't need to know," he interrupted. "Just

understand it's appreciated. Now come with me. I know a little café that has amazing coffee, and I'd like to spend the afternoon with you."

Catherine didn't push, and neither did he. She let him lead her to the café and the afternoon of laughter that followed. Maybe she'd needed Ash as much as he'd needed her. Fate had a funny way of stepping in that way.

Thank you so much for taking the time to read my book.
Your opinion matters!
Please take a moment to review this book on your favorite review site and share your opinion with fellow readers.

www.authordawnbrower.com

www.ingramcontent.com/pod-product-compliance
Lightning Source LLC
Chambersburg PA
CBHW031129160726
47989CB00017B/2517